Weekly Reader Books presents

★ ALAN COREN ★

RAILROAD ARTHUR

Illustrated by John Astrop

Little, Brown and Company
Boston   Toronto

REPRINTED BY ARRANGEMENT WITH LITTLE, BROWN AND COMPANY, INC.

Library of Congress Cataloging in Publication Data

Coren, Alan, 1938–
  Railroad Arthur.

  SUMMARY: Ten-year-old Arthur must not only solve a
series of train robberies but must clear his own name
of suspicion.
  [1. Railroads—Trains—Fiction. 2. Robbers and
outlaws—Fiction. 3. The West—Fiction] I. Astrop,
John. II. Title.
PZ7.C81538Rai   1977   [Fic]   77-28419
ISBN 0-316-15736-8

This book is a presentation of
Weekly Reader Books.

Weekly Reader Books offers book clubs for children
from preschool through junior high school.
All quality hardcover books are selected by
a distinguished Weekly Reader Selection Board.

For further information write to:
Weekly Reader Books
1250 Fairwood Ave.
Columbus, Ohio 43216

PRINTED IN THE UNITED STATES OF AMERICA

For Elinor

★

ONCE upon a time, about a hundred years ago, in the very middle of the state of Kansas, which itself is in the very middle of the United States, stood the railroad station of Junction City.

Junction City had not, of course, always been called that. Up until only five years before, it had been called Dead Pig Bend, and it had been a very small town indeed. As a matter of fact, it had been called Dead Pig Bend *because* it was a very small town indeed, just four tiny wooden houses standing in the corners of four very tiny and very poor farms. The four families who lived there had never had a name for the place at all until the pig belonging to one of them had suddenly dropped dead one day. This was considered to be so impor-

tant an event in this tiny community that they decided to commemorate it by naming the town after what had happened.

So Dead Pig Bend it remained until the day the railroad came.

It would not be accurate to say that the railroad came *to* Dead Pig Bend, because quite obviously nobody would take the trouble to build a railway across hundreds of miles of country just to get to a place where the most important thing that had ever happened was a dead pig. The railroad came *through* Dead Pig Bend, so that very large and important towns in the West could be connected to very large and important towns in the East, and since

Dead Pig Bend was bang in the middle of North America, it suddenly found itself bang in the middle of the railroad.

And because, very soon after that, another railroad was laid connecting important places in the North with important places in the South which also went slap through the middle of Dead Pig Bend, the town became a junction. So what was more natural than to rename it Junction City, which sounded so much grander than Dead Pig Bend?

Junction City was very grand indeed. With the coming of the railroad, the little town had suddenly exploded into a city of more than three hundred houses, many of them brick, and even one or two with four floors! And if that doesn't sound quite as grand as a modern city, well, don't forget that this was 1875, when America was still pretty new and when a city of three hundred houses in the middle of the wide Kansas plains was something to be very proud of.

Particularly when its railroad station was generally reckoned to be the finest for a thousand miles in any direction! It had not merely four wide white platforms, two ticket offices lit by bright yellow gaslight, a gentlemen's waiting-room so enormous that in winter it required a roaring fire *at each end*, and a ladies' waiting-room so elegant that a Russian princess once stopped her private train at Junction City just to look at it; it also had a magnificent canary yellow bell tower that rose high above every other building in the town and bonged the approach of trains so loudly and so clearly that cattle on ranches ten miles away would suddenly stop chewing, look up, and moo whenever the echoing clang rolled across the green countryside.

Nor, indeed, was the station any less of a landmark by night, when the glow from its welding shop lit the sky and when the grunt of shunting trucks and the screech of iron wheels and the slamming of carriage doors would keep the townspeople turning in their beds. They did not wake, though, for they were used to the rolling thunder of the trains. It was in their dreams that they turned, dreams that were full of the magic of bright wheels clattering them to fine, far, fabulous places of which they had so far only heard, but which they would, they now knew, someday see.

And there was one more feature of Junction City station, which in this story is very important indeed.

It had a bridge.

Canary yellow, to match the bell tower, the bridge straddled the tracks and the platforms so that travelers could cross from one side of the station to the other; and if you stood in the middle of that bridge, you were standing pretty well in the very center of the United

5

States of America, with the tracks stretching away from beneath your feet until they seemed to disappear in the soft shimmer of the far horizons. It could give you a rather strange feeling in your stomach; it could make your heart beat just a bit faster. Many people who crossed that bridge would stop, and look, and feel the odd feeling; and after they had gone on, they would remember the sensation for a very long time afterward.

On the day upon which this story begins, a boy about ten years old had been standing there all morning. Later, after everything had happened, the townspeople found that they couldn't remember when they had first noticed him. Certainly, nobody knew where he had come from. But as the warm sun rose into that spring morning a hundred years ago, there he was, leaning on the yellow rail of the bridge, staring westward down the line, and occasionally writing something in a large red notebook, very carefully and seriously.

It was the stationmaster who first spoke to him. Mr. Beesley was an important man (though not, perhaps, *quite* as important as he thought he was). He took his position very seriously, and he liked to know about such details as small boys standing on what he considered to be his bridge for unusual lengths of time. So, toward noon, Mr. Beesley walked, very importantly, up the steps and into the middle of the bridge. He cleared his throat, and tweaked his bow tie with green polka dots, and put his hands behind his back, and said: "What are you doing, boy?"

The boy looked up.

"I am collecting train numbers," he said.

Mr. Beesley didn't quite know what to say. He was the sort of man who tended to think that anything boys did was bound to be wrong and even more bound to be silly.

"Why?" he said at last, very suspiciously.

"Because," said the boy, "it's my hobby. I take down the number of every train that goes past."

"I've never heard anything like it in my life," snorted Mr. Beesley.

"That is probably because I'm the first person who's ever collected them," said the boy, firmly but politely. "Do you mind?"

If the truth were known, Mr. Beesley did mind. He didn't know why he minded. He had a vague notion it was because he didn't want boys cluttering up his beautiful station, but he couldn't be absolutely certain, and since he was a man who liked to be absolutely certain of everything (which was why, of course, he had been put in charge of trains), he felt he couldn't actually do anything about the boy. So he merely humphed and snorted a bit, and said,

"Well, don't try ANYTHING!" very sternly, and walked away again, back toward the steps.

He was half-way down when he heard "Look at *that!*"

He turned and came quickly back up the steps, hoping that the boy might have done something which would give him the chance to remove him.

"What is it?" snapped Mr. Beesley.

The boy pointed. The stationmaster wasn't usually in the habit of taking any notice when boys pointed, but he couldn't help himself; and when he looked, he staggered!

Up the westward track, about a mile away but coming toward them fast, was a train. Nothing odd about that, you'll say: except that it was coming *backward*, the caboose leading the way, and the engine hurtling along in reverse, its black smoke blotching the pale noon sky!

"That's the eleven-fifteen to Dooley Flat!" cried the boy. "It left here less than an hour ago!"

"*I* know that!" snapped the distraught sta-

9

tionmaster, over his shoulder, running as fast as his little plump legs would go.

The strange train came on, hooting frantically as it came. No sooner had it braked to a shrieking stop beside the platform than every door opened simultaneously and passengers shot out as if from catapults and began running around shouting, waving, and generally behaving in a very extraordinary manner indeed. Spotting Mr. Beesley, they converged, swarmed, leaped, until he disappeared, wriggling out on all fours some moments later with the green-dotted bow tie under one ear and his broken top hat jammed down over his eyes.

The assistant stationmaster, who was called Herbert McPhoon and who was so thin and so worried that Junction City was divided into those people who thought he was thin because he worried and those who thought he worried because he was thin, came galloping up on his long spindly legs and began wringing his hands.

"Oh, Mr. Beesley!" he cried. "Backward! The eleven-fifteen has come in again, back-

ward! However shall we explain it to the company?"

"Shut up, McPhoon!" cried the stationmaster. "Get me out of this hat!"

Herbert McPhoon, noticing the smashed hat for the first time, shrieked.

"Your hat, Mr. Beesley!" he cried. "Your official stationmaster's hat is ruined! We have a wrecked hat on our hands! However shall we explain it to the company?"

"Just pull, you fool!" roared Mr. Beesley, and his assistant pulled, and Mr. Beesley pulled, and at last, with a noise not unlike that of a cork popping from a bottle, the station-master's head came clear. McPhoon held the shattered hat in his trembling hands and stared at it.

"Beyond repair!" he moaned.

Mr. Beesley snatched it from him and hurled it aside.

"Never mind the darned hat, McPhoon!" he shouted. "There's been a robbery!"

His assistant reeled.

"The passengers!" he exclaimed. "I saw them climbing all over you. I remember thinking: *They're climbing all over Mr. Beesley, however shall we explain it to the company?* What did they steal? Oh, don't say it's your gold company watch with *Property of the Kansas & Missouri Railroad* engraved on it, however shall we explain it to . . ."

"IT AIN'T ME WHAT'S BEEN ROBBED!" yelled

Mr. Beesley, his temper ruining his usually perfect grammar. "IT IS THE TRAIN!"

Herbert McPhoon fainted.

★

It was true. A mere ten miles up the line, a large log had been laid across the tracks. The driver had stopped, and, quick as fish darting from beneath a stone, half a dozen robbers had sprung from cover, overpowered the cab crew, and escaped with not only twenty mailbags but also every single valuable from every single passenger.

They filed past Mr. Beesley's big gleaming desk, these poor travelers, giving the sad details, many of them forced to hold up the trousers from which the gold-buckled belts had been grabbed or mopping their faces with cravats from which the diamond stickpins had been wickedly plucked. As they moped past, Herbert McPhoon took down the losses while Mr. Beesley called them out. From time to time, Herbert McPhoon would have to stop to mop up the page onto which one of his many huge tears had just fallen; he had never been so worried in his entire life before.

"All those mailbags!" he wailed, as the last passenger filed out. "Imagine wanting to read other people's letters, Mr. Beesley! I've never heard anything so rude in all my born days."

Mr. Beesley stared at him.

"McPhoon, sometimes I . . ."

15

He stopped. Red-eyed, Herbert McPhoon looked up.

"Yes, Mr. Beesley?"

The stationmaster shook his head, and his second-best hat, too large for him by several sizes, bobbed and wiggled.

"Nothing, McPhoon, nothing." He sighed. "It wasn't the letters, laddie; those bags contained thousands of dollars!"

Herbert McPhoon's mouth opened in horror, but no words came out of it. Up above his mouth, inside his head, Herbert McPhoon was thinking of all the bosses of the company, stone-faced men with glittering eyes and thin sharp lips, who would be coming down and Asking Questions. And, almost certainly, Firing People.

"Whatever shall become of us, Mr. Beesley?" he managed to whisper, at last.

"I think you ought to have a plan," said a voice.

The two men looked round. The voice seemed to come from low down.

"It's that blessed boy from the bridge!" snapped the stationmaster.

"What boy?" cried Herbert McPhoon, growing typically even more worried. "Which bridge?"

"My name," said the boy, "is Arthur. I stand on your bridge, most days."

"He stands on our bridge most days!" shrieked Herbert McPhoon. "However shall we explain it to the company?"

"You've got more than that to explain to the company," said Arthur sternly. "I bet a lot of people are going to be asking questions about how your train got robbed in broad daylight."

"THAT IS NONE OF YOUR BUSINESS!" shouted Mr. Beesley.

"Oh, yes, it is," replied Arthur; but very politely. He was not a boy to answer back unless the matter was very important. "I'll just bet that unless you start taking what are called Special Precautions, there'll be more robberies. The next thing you know, people will stop using Junction City, or even stop using trains altogether, and quite apart from the fact that that will foul up my train-spotting and leave my book without lots of numbers I ought to have, it will be a black day for the train business. *And*," he added, with a dark look that made Herbert McPhoon shiver, "it will be a black day for America, too!"

The stationmaster gasped! Nobody had ever dared lecture *him* about trains, let alone a boy of ten.

"Get him out of here, McPhoon!" he cried.

But the dark look was still in Arthur's eyes. Even though he was small, there was Something about him which froze Herbert McPhoon where he stood.

"There is no need," said Arthur, quietly, "for force. There rarely is." And, tucking his red notebook under his arm, he left.

Arthur was right.

The sheriff of Junction City was, naturally, informed of the robbery; but Mr. Beesley, fearing that too large a fuss would panic passengers, insisted that the whole business be handled quietly and a reasonable explanation for the incident be found.

Nothing could have better suited the sheriff, who had ridden out with two deputies (Mr. Beesley having pointed out that a posse would only alarm people unnecessarily) and found no clues whatever. It has to be said, I'm afraid, that he was neither a very bright nor a very brave sheriff. Junction City was not a cow town nor a frontier town; it had never had any trouble with wild cowboys or dangerous gunslingers. It was a respectable business town, in the respectable business of railway management, and all it required of its sheriff was that he be respectable. It had no use for a lean mean man who wore his six guns low and could shoot the ears off a baddie from fifty paces. It wanted a sheriff who wore a smart suit and a fashionable hat and permanently polished boots, who went to church regularly and drank nothing stronger than tea (and never out of the saucer), a man who never swore or played cards for money or picked his ear with a matchstick, the way tough Western sheriffs tended to. It wanted a sheriff, in short, who would give Junction City what is called *tone*.

And it had one. I have to tell you that it wasn't just because he wasn't much of a detective that he didn't find clues at the scene of the robbery. It was also because he rather preferred *not* to find clues, just in case they led to the bad men who had left them, which might have ended in a gunfight, causing damage not only to his smart suit, his fine hat, and his shiny boots, but also to him.

So he came back and announced to the town that he had decided that the robbers had got clear away to the next state, where he was not, much to his regret, allowed to pursue them. The railroad company simultaneously announced that it would compensate the passengers for what they had lost, and everybody was happy.

For two days.

Because, on the third day, and just as Arthur had predicted, the nine-forty-five to Catsmeat Creek came backward up the line again. Twenty five miles from Junction City, as the train halted briefly to take on water, a masked gang had leaped from behind the water tank and got away with another dozen mailbags, plus, again, all the personal valuables of the passengers, who an hour later were jumping up and down on Platform Two and screaming at the unfortunate Mr. Beesley and his weeping assistant, Herbert McPhoon.

"Catch them!" wailed a short lady, who would not have been quite so short had the robbers not stolen, in addition to her emerald earrings, her best shoes.

"Stop them!" shouted a man in a *Kansas & Missouri Railroad* towel, this being the first thing he had grabbed when his Sunday suit with the twelve gold buttons had disappeared into the robbers' sack.

"Shoot them!" yelled the manager of the First National Bank of Junction City, who looked as though he might have shot Mr. Beesley, had the robbers not stolen his solid silver pearl-handled revolvers, which, unfortunately, his wife had never allowed him to load in case he hurt somebody.

"HOWEVER SHALL WE EXPLAIN IT TO THE COMPANY?" shrieked Herbert McPhoon, who was running around in small circles, pulling his ginger hair.

"I think you ought to have a plan," said a
voice.

Everyone fell silent.

"Who said that?" inquired the bank manager.

"I did," said Arthur.

"You again!" exclaimed Mr. Beesley. "I thought I told you never to interfere! I've a good mind to stop you standing on my bridge."

"*Our* bridge, you mean," corrected the bank manager, shooting a look at the stationmaster which made Mr. Beesley mumble and sniff and stare at his shoes. "Why do you stand on our bridge, boy?"

Arthur didn't much care for people who called him "boy." Apart from the fact that they tended to be people with red faces and loud voices who threw their weight around in a generally disagreeable manner, he felt it was a sign of bad manners. He, after all, didn't go about calling people "man" or "woman." So he said: "It's my bridge, too, you know. But, since you ask, I collect train numbers."

"Rubbish!" cried the bank manager. "Pack of lies! Who in his right mind would collect train numbers? Can't eat train numbers, can you? Can't sell train numbers? Where's the profit in train numbers?"

"Oh, there's no profit," replied Arthur. "It's just that I —"

"Boy's a fool!" said the bank manager.

And I'm sorry to have to say that everyone present agreed.

"Well, I think we ought to have a plan," announced the bank manager, when they'd all finished nodding.

"What a marvelous idea!" cried everyone. Arthur didn't say anything; it would have been extremely rude to have said "I said that two days ago" or something like that. Anyway, he was worried about what was happening to the trains, and he didn't care who came up with a plan, just as long as someone did.

"I think," said the bank manager, who

seemed to have turned himself into a leader, which was probably the reason Mr. Beesley was glaring at him from beneath his wobbly hat with eyes red and hot as poker ends, "I think we ought to put armed guards on all the trains."

"It'll panic the passengers," protested Mr. Beesley.

"Better than being robbed," said the bank manager.

"Yuggle," agreed a short fat man whose entire set of gold teeth had been stolen and who now, in consequence, had great difficulty in getting his words out properly. "Beggle thaggle biggle robbie!"

"Twenty-three trains pass through here

every day," said Arthur, who had been consulting his red notebook, "and you'd need at least six guards per train. That makes one hundred and thirty-eight guards."

They all looked at him, astounded. They had never heard mental arithmetic like it. Most of them, it has to be said, couldn't have counted up to twenty without taking their shoes off. Naturally, this made them even more angry with Arthur; you know what people are like sometimes.

"This is none of your business!" cried Mr. Beesley.

"Nuggle of yoggle biggle!" cried the short fat man.

"One guard per train is ample," announced the bank manager. "All baddies are cowards. It is a well-known fact. The sight of one guard will be enough."

"Right!" interjected Mr. Beesley, who thought it was about time he said something before those present started forgetting it was his station. "And we shall draw our guards from the railway employees so as not to startle passengers with a lot of armed strangers all over the place. *I* shall supervise it!"

It was not the plan which Arthur had in mind at all. Not to mince words, Arthur reckoned it was just about the worst plan he had ever heard. What they ought to have been working on was a plan not merely to stop any further robberies, but also to recover all the money and valuables that had been stolen, catch the robbers into the bargain, *and* bring them to justice, because bringing criminals to justice was what law was all about. He would have pointed this out had anyone asked him, but since they hadn't, he thought it best not to volunteer his opinion. Arthur knew enough about the townspeople of Junction City by now to have a pretty good idea of just how far *that* would have got him.

The sheriff, of course, rode out once more to the scene of the crime; and the sheriff, of course, rode back once more with no more evidence than on the previous occasion. In fact, this time he didn't even dismount. It had rained and the trackside was thick with wet mud, and he was wearing a pair of hand-tooled boots with real silver spurs he had ordered specially from the most expensive shop in Kansas City, and the last thing he wanted all over them was mud.

Thus it was that the bank manager's plan was put into operation. And, sure enough, two days later, Arthur from his vantage point on the canary yellow bridge was the first person to see the ten-thirty to Peanut Falls chugging as fast as it could chug toward Junction City.

Backward.

In all the shouting and weeping and accusing and apologizing that followed in the stationmaster's office, it transpired that the railway employee who had been put aboard that particular train had been, of all people, Herbert McPhoon. True, he had been wearing two large and impressive-looking .44 Colt Special revolvers and carrying an even more impressive-looking 12-gauge Spencer shotgun loaded with enough steel shot to blow a hole in the side of the train, but the trouble was

that that was exactly what the unfortunate Herbert McPhoon did with it. Thirty miles from Junction City, a black-and-white cow had wandered onto the line. The train engineer, who had been brought up to be kind to animals, stopped the train and went to lead the cow off the tracks; but as soon as he approached, the cow had removed its head to reveal an extremely nasty-looking outlaw, and immediately afterward removed its bottom to reveal an even nastier-looking one.

Whereupon four more men appeared from the bushes on either side of the line, and the six desperadoes leapt aboard the train, firing into the roof and requesting that the passengers turn over all they had.

At the first shot, Herbert McPhoon, who had, I'm afraid to say, been daydreaming, worrying about whether his mother would remember to feed his goldfish, jumped to his feet in the mail car so suddenly that the shotgun across his knees went off. It blew out a hole just large enough for two of the robbers to climb through, shout "BOO!" at him so that he immediately fainted, and steal the twenty-five mailbags on which Herbert McPhoon had been dozing.

It was as this awful story came to its end, and Mr. Beesley began slapping his weeping assistant with the green flag he always carried, that a voice from the back of the room said: "I knew that would happen."

Everyone looked round. There was no sound at all, save the sad sniveling of Herbert McPhoon. Arthur looked up from his large red notebook; and, since no one had yet replied, said: "Well, I *did!*"

Mr. Beesley advanced down the crowded room toward him.

Now, you have to remember that Mr. Beesley had had a very bad week. Every two days, a train pulling out of his station had been robbed. The whole town was not only holding him responsible, it was also telling him what to do, and, worse, muttering behind his back that perhaps it was about time Junction City found a new stationmaster. Added to which, the *Kansas & Missouri Railroad* was beginning to say the same and *they* hadn't even learned of the third robbery yet.

You may have noticed that when someone suddenly starts getting blamed for everything that goes wrong, he often tries to fight back by laying the blame on somebody else.

Which was exactly the case with Mr. Beesley.

Without really thinking what he was saying at all, he glared down at Arthur, pointed his long angry finger at him, and roared:

"SO YOU KNEW THAT WOULD HAPPEN, DID

33

YOU? WELL, THAT DOESN'T SURPRISE ME ONE LITTLE BIT! I THINK YOU'RE MIXED UP IN IT!"

A buzz ran round the crowded room, first a murmur, then a din, because everybody had an opinion, and everybody thought that Mr. Beesley must know what he was talking about. Then a hand grabbed Arthur's red notebook, and a voice yelled: "Hey, look here, he's been taking down the numbers of all the trains!"

Before Arthur could tell them that that was

what he had explained to them ages ago, they were beginning to remark that this was very suspicious indeed. He had doubtless been spying for the robbers, that was why he had listened in on all their conversations; the robbers had used him just because they reckoned a boy of ten wouldn't arouse suspicion, and so on, and so on, until they'd all managed to persuade themselves that Arthur was the very *leader* of the railroad gang, that he was probably known as Railroad Arthur, that he was probably wanted in seven states . . .

"I knew it all along!" cried the bank manager. "*You* were all taken in! Collecting train numbers indeed! Ha and double ha! *Sheriff, arrest that boy!*"

There is every chance that had Arthur been grown-up, the sheriff would not have dared to do anything of the sort. But, having taken a long careful look at Arthur from behind an old lady, and having assured himself that he was a small boy, and having examined him very carefully for dangerous weapons such as guns, or catapults, or even a stick that might give you a nasty poke and tear your best silk shirt, and not been able to spot any, the sheriff drew himself up to his full height, took his gun from its beautiful holster (it was the first time it had ever left it), and declared: "Railroad Arthur, I arrest you on suspicion of train robbery!"

"Don't be silly," said Arthur.

"And of being rude to a grown-up!" roared the sheriff.

"You can't arrest me for that," said Arthur, "and I had absolutely nothing to do with the robberies."

"That proves it!" cried Mr. Beesley. "He's denying it! Did you ever hear of a crook who *didn't* deny what he'd done?"

"Lock him up!" cried the crowd.

There really wasn't a great deal Arthur could do, after that. So he sighed, and shrugged, and took the whole thing very bravely, as was his way. He gave them one of his sternest looks, and began to walk out in front of the sheriff with his hands in the air. But he stopped at the door, and turned.

"You're all going to look awfully silly at the trial," he said.

But the more he thought about it, the less certain he grew that this would in fact be so. True, there wasn't much evidence against him; but, then again, there wasn't much evidence *for* him, and Arthur knew enough about Western trials, and Western judges, and Western law in general to know that half the people in prison had done nothing worse than make enemies of people like Mr. Beesley and the bank manager and the sheriff. After all, he was only a boy, and they were pretty important people. So whom would the judge and jury believe?

He had a lot of time to think all this out. There wasn't much to do in prison. You either sat on the bed and looked at the stool, or you sat on the stool and looked at the bed. He wasn't tall enough to see out of the little barred window, and it didn't take long to eat the cold stew he was given for lunch or the stale bread

and dusty water he was given for supper. So he sat and thought.

He would have to prove he had nothing to do with the crimes. And to do that, he would have to prove who did. That would have been almost impossible if he'd been free, and was completely impossible now that he was stuck in jail. But — and his mind kept returning to it — only *almost* impossible if he were free; because, while Arthur had no idea who the robbers were, he did know something which nobody else knew.

He knew which of the forty-six trains that went through Junction City every two days they had robbed, and he knew what each of those three trains they had selected from the 138 possibilities had in common.

And if he was right, then he knew exactly which train they would rob in the *next* two days, if they struck again. The trouble was, he couldn't tell anyone this. Since the whole town was now convinced that he was the brains behind the gang, they would not be at all surprised if he told them which train was going to be robbed next. In fact, they'd take it as *proof* that he was in with the robbers and was squealing on them just to save his own skin!

Worse still, they might even think his plan was to get the gang caught, thus making everyone believe he was innocent, so that when he was set free he could take all the loot for himself!

His only course, Arthur realized, was not only to capture the robbers but also to get all the stolen property back. There was no way *that* would happen if he simply told Mr. Beesley which train was going to be robbed. Mr. Beesley would fill it with armed guards, and if that happened the guards would only either shoot the robbers or capture them. They would never find the outlaws' hideout where the loot was kept; and unless they did, everyone would still suspect Arthur of being mixed up in it.

It was all incredibly complicated.

Until Arthur had his idea.

He was halfway through the awful stew when he had it; and, do you know, it was such a remarkable idea that he actually finished his stew, without even noticing, while he was working it out?

It was (and although Arthur never boasted, not even to himself, he had to admit that it was) a brilliant and daring idea. Unfortunately,

like so many brilliant and daring ideas, it was
also such a frightening one that it made the
small hairs on the back of his neck tingle and
his mouth go rather dry.

But don't think that deterred Arthur for one
moment!

The main problem was that, in order to put
his great plan into operation, he had to escape
from jail. He hadn't considered escaping before, because he'd reckoned that if he did try
to get out everyone would take it as even more
solid proof that he was guilty. But now he had
to think about it; and because the next train
due to be robbed was the following morning's

nine-thirty to Weasel Fork, he had to think quickly.

The window was out; too high on the wall, and barred by a fine grille. The door was thick iron bars, built so strong that not even the most powerful man could bend them an inch. The lock was a new blue-steel triple-barred affair. And as for overpowering the sheriff when he came to bring him his food, that might possibly have worked for a desperate outlaw, but it was obviously not the sort of fight that even the toughest ten-year-old boy was likely to win.

It seemed hopeless.

But Arthur never used words like *hopeless*. Arthur used his brains instead, figuring that if only you thought hard enough and carefully enough, you could always find a solution, no matter how enormous the problem.

So he thought; and while he thought, he looked at the window and the door and the lock, because from one of them the solution would come. He kept repeating to himself what he had said about them, since what he had said had been the first things that had come into his head, and he knew there would be second things there, if only . . .

When it came, the answer was so obvious, he fell back on the hard little bed and kicked his feet in the air! *Not even the most powerful man could bend the bars an inch* had been his first thought, hadn't it? And it had been the first thought of the man who had built the jail: make it so strong that no man alive could break out!

No *man* alive. He hadn't even considered the possibility of keeping in a boy; because, obviously, anything built to hold a man would hold a boy.

Except that boys are a lot smaller than men.

Which was why Arthur slid off the bed, heart pounding, and tiptoed to the bars, breathed in, prayed, then put one leg out into the corridor, and one arm, and then his body, and last, with a rather painful squeeze, his head.

And stood in the corridor!

Quickly, he squeezed back inside his cell to wait for nightfall. He thanked his lucky stars

that he was not a grown man, but a ten-year-
old boy. And, because he had never been
greedy, a pretty slim one, at that!

★

Arthur heard the far door slam as the sheriff, whistling, went off for supper. He listened for a few minutes, just to make sure the sheriff wasn't coming back, then squeezed out through the bars and went quickly into the outer office. His knife and his string and his red notebook were on the sheriff's rolltop desk. He took a swift glance inside the book, just to be absolutely certain that the doomed train *was* the nine-thirty to Weasel Fork, then pocketed his knife and his string and slipped out, through the back door, into the night.

Keeping in the shadows, Arthur moved noiselessly along the backs of the buildings until he reached the end of Main Street and there was nothing between him and the station but a rather unnervingly large and well-lit open square. Luckily, it being suppertime, there was nobody around; so Arthur took a deep breath, and ran.

He did not stop until he reached the back of the Mail Office. Carefully, he pulled him-

45

self up onto the windowsill, looked inside, and confirmed that the room was piled with mail-bags waiting for dispatch. All that remained — and it was a pretty big All! — was to find a way to get inside and join them.

The windows were, of course, barred: and the front door, he knew, was not only locked but guarded. It was time, Arthur realized, for some more hard thinking!

He eased himself up on the windowsill once more, to see if perhaps one of the bars wasn't loose; none was, but while he was up there, he noticed something which set him thinking. In one corner of the room was a large wicker basket, marked LIVESTOCK: HANDLE WITH CARE. There must, thought Arthur, be chickens in there, and if there are chickens . . .

He dropped to the ground, and peered about. A few yards off stood one of the station horse troughs, and beside it, as luck would have it, was an old wooden bucket. He ran to it, crouching, filled the bucket with water, and ran, still crouching, back into the shadow of the wall.

Now came the tricky part.

Not to say the bravest part, too.

Arthur took off his spectacles and put them carefully into his shirt pocket. It was quite surprising how different he looked without his glasses. Then he smeared mud all over his face and his clothes, partly because that made him look even more unlike his normal very neat self, and partly because, especially after he had taken his shoes off and hidden them inside his shirt and rolled his trousers up to the knee, that made him look much more like a rather dirty farm boy. This done, he picked up his bucket, and, whistling cheerfully, walked around to the front of the building.

Right up to the guard!

"Hello!" cried Arthur, in a specially disguised voice. "Open up!"

"Can't go in there, sonny," said the tall guard, gruffly.

"Got to water me dad's chickens!" protested Arthur. "They'll be dead before morning if I don't."

The guard looked at him. It seemed to Arthur that he looked at him for about an hour, but, of course, that was only because it was a pretty terrifying experience.

"Okay," said the guard, at last, "but be quick, and don't touch nothing!"

Arthur made a mental note to tell the guard, when this business was all over, and in, of course, the nicest possible way, that he should have said "Don't touch anything," and, as soon as the door was unlocked, strode boldly into the Mail Office.

"I'll just close the door," he called to the guard, "in case one of the chickens tries to escape."

He lost not a second. Quickly, he found the pile of mailbags with URGENT: WEASEL FORK stenciled on them. He hid the bucket in the farthest corner of the room. And then, having rolled down his trousers, put his shoes back on, wiped his face, and replaced his spectacles, he put into immediate operation part one of his Plan!

Ten minutes later, the guard came into the room.

"About time you were out of here, kid!" he said.

There was no reply.

"BOY!" called the guard.

He walked around the room, peering to left and right, scratching his jaw.

"Must've slipped out without my noticing,"

he murmured aloud. "And not even a thank you. Boys these days!"

Inside his mailbag, Arthur allowed himself a little private grin.

He was being dragged along, upside down, his head bumping the hard floor.

Painful as it was, at least it woke him up.

"Heavy one here, Charlie!" called a voice, and the next moment Arthur felt his head coming up as another pair of hands lifted his bag clear of the ground.

Then he was flying through the air!

He tensed himself for the crash, but luckily it never came. He landed instead on something lumpy, yet thankfully soft; the rest of the mail, thought Arthur.

"I see that kid escaped in the night," called the first voice, farther off now.

"Yeah," replied a second. "Knew he was a wrong 'un all along! They say the rest of the gang rode into town during the night and unlocked his cell."

"Had to be," said the first voice. "Nobody breaks out of Junction City jail! Finest clink in the state!"

Amazing, reflected Arthur, how people would always believe anything, if only they wanted to enough.

"We'll get him, though," said the second voice nastily. "And when we do . . ."

They both laughed, and Arthur suddenly felt, despite the warmth of the spring morning, very cold indeed. His plan had better work.

He heard the heavy steel doors of the car begin to roll together, but just before they slammed shut, the first voice spoke again:

"Hold on there, Charlie! Gotta wait for the guard."

"Been a change of plan," said the second voice. "Got two guards traveling up front on the engine. Train's not gonna stop for anything, and first sign of trouble she's gonna drive straight on with full steam up and both guards blasting away! Not a horse been born that can outrun this old engine!"

The doors clanged together, and the huge bolts slid home.

Arthur wasn't too happy about what he had just heard. This could ruin his plan completely! The gang would attack the train, of that he was certain, but if they didn't succeed in stopping it, his whole scheme was done for.

And, to make matters immeasurably worse, he would then end up in Weasel Fork, four hundred miles away, an escaped prisoner wanted for mail robbery *and caught in a mailbag!*

There, in the sack-smelling dark, jolting along as the train gathered speed out of Junction City, Arthur prayed, for the first time in his life, for something really wicked to happen. He prayed that the railroad gang would succeed! He felt, at that moment, extremely alone; his bravery was getting a pretty tough test, all things considered.

Across the floor of the car, the chickens in their basket, as if sensing that they were off to Weasel Fork to end up as somebody's dinner, suddenly burst out into frantic clucking.

Arthur knew just how they felt.

On and on clacketed the train, gathering speed across the flatlands, mile after mile after mile — too many miles, thought Arthur after perhaps half an hour. If the gang was going to attack it would have done so by now. Junction City must have been thirty-five miles behind. They had passed all the best ambush points; perhaps the gang had spotted the two armed men up front, perhaps they had heard about the new plan to stop for nothing — there were a thousand reasons why they might have decided enough was enough, and left the territory.

He felt the train slow down, slightly at first, then more markedly; it must, thought Arthur, be going up the long incline outside Plumville. And so it was, the great engine straining, the bright orange coaches strung out behind, the heavy mail car with its strange load of money and chickens and Arthur bringing up the rear.

And then, quite simply, it stopped!

Not the whole train.

Just the boxcar.

Only for a second; for, hardly had it stopped than it started to run again, backward this time, down the hill! Just before it changed direction, Arthur had heard a clink, and a rasp, and a clang, and he had not been sure what the noise was at the time, but now, a second later, he was very sure indeed — someone had uncoupled the mail car from the train!

It was hurtling back down the hill, gathering

speed with every passing second, while the rest of the train steamed obstinately on ahead!

Arthur curled himself into as tight a ball as he could, digging himself deeper into the surrounding mailbags against the shock of the impending crash; one of the gang must have got on board at Junction City, quietly worked his way to the end of the train, slipped the coupling on the last coach, and . . .

You had to admit, thought Arthur (even though he had quite a lot of other things on his mind in those hurtling seconds), it was a pretty daring and a pretty crafty gang, all right!

Faster and faster sped the car, swaying horribly, the cargo sliding around and crashing into the walls, the chickens cackling even above the din of grinding and creaking steel, and Arthur there in his private darkness, teeth and fists clenched and eyes tight shut against the impact, not daring to imagine what was about to happen. Any minute now, any second, any moment . . .

The crash never came. Miraculously, the swaying baggage car stayed upright on the rails, gradually lurching less, slowing little by little, settling into a quieter and quieter pace, until, very gently, it stopped.

Silence. Even the chickens seemed to have been stunned by their incredible escape and run out of things to say. Arthur, who suddenly realized he had been holding his breath ever since the car had started its mad backward career, now let it out in a low hissing gasp.

Then he heard hooves, approaching rapidly, and shouting voices, and men reining in and dismounting. Then a lone rider galloped up, who must have been, guessed Arthur, the man who had uncoupled the car and then jumped from the slowing train to his waiting horse.

He heard crowbars rasp against the padlocked bolts, the crack as the steel snapped, and the rumble as the doors flew open. He kept his head and made himself go limp, though his heartbeat banged in his ears as he felt rough hands grasp his mailbag and drag it out of the van. He just hoped they wouldn't break the seals that had been put on when the bag had been stapled together at Junction City that morning and try to get at the contents on the spot; his whole plan had depended, from the very start, on the guess that the robbers would want to get away from the scene of the crime as fast as possible and not open the bags until they'd arrived at their hideout.

He had, as usual with Arthur, guessed right. He felt his bag being tied at the neck to another, and next thing he knew, the pair had been slung behind a saddle, and he was off, bumping horribly against the flank of the horse as its rider spurred it to top speed.

How long they galloped, Arthur couldn't begin to guess: his whole mind and body was concentrating on staying in one piece and not yelling out with the fearful battering he was taking. All he knew was that after an interminable agony of high-speed racing, the horse slowed, and picked its way stumblingly upward. A few minutes later, his bag was dragged to the ground; and as he lay there, bruised and aching all over, he heard the sound of other bags falling, other horses snorting their fatigue, and men laughing low laughs, whooping and slapping each other's backs.

He was there, in the very heart of the train gang's camp!

Would they give him the precious few seconds he needed?

Or would their greed and inquisitiveness, as well they might, urge them to rip the bags apart straight away to get at their loot? That was the terrible gamble Arthur had taken all along. Would he have the long moment necessary to cut himself out of his bag, escape from the gang undetected, somehow get to the nearest place to summon help (and heaven only knew where *that* might be!), and lead the law back to deal with the gang before the villains had realized that anything was amiss?

And then, suddenly, his insides went cold!

"C'mon, boys, let's open our presents from the railroad!" roared a terrible voice.

It was all up!

Arthur tensed for discovery and an unimaginable fate!

And then:

"Them bags ain't going nowhere," cried another voice. "We been riding like hell was opening behind us; I say we take a drink!"

"I say we take ten drinks!" cried a third voice, and when the others cheered, Arthur breathed again. He heard the jangle of their spurs as the robbers moved away from the pile of bags. When he heard them guzzling noisily and laughing, very, very carefully he took his clasp-knife from his pocket, opened it, jabbed a small hole in his sack, and began, inch by delicate inch, to slit it open.

After he had made the cut, he lay still, waiting. One eye to the opening, he peeped, and saw that it was dark outside. A cave, he thought gratefully and, very gently, began to ease himself out through the hole.

Luckily, his sack was on the side of the heap away from the gang. Pressed flat, moving like the most cautious snake, Arthur wriggled across the gritty floor of the cave and behind a boulder. Realizing that they would not be able to make him out in the dark depth of the cave, Arthur now looked round the boulder's edge. The six villains were on their haunches in the cave mouth, thick black silhouettes against the bright triangle of sky, swigging from their bottles like figures in a shadow play.

There was no way on earth that he could get past them!

At the very last moment, poised before the final hurdle, the Great Plan had failed.

They did not drink for long: the bottles were sucked dry, thrown down, smashed, and the six badmen stood up, their joined mass blocking the light, and began to move down the cave toward him.

At the pile of bulging sacks, they stopped; knives flashed from their sheaths. And then, as they were about to plunge among the bags, one of the robbers let out the most thunderous roar!

"WHAT THE . . . ONE OF YOU SCUM HAS BEEN AT THE BAGS ALREADY!"

He — it must, thought Arthur, be the leader — held up the ripped remnants of

Arthur's sack. His eyes, as he swiveled around, licked like flames at the darkness. But when he spoke again, his voice was horribly, chillingly low:

"Was it you, Slimy Sid?"

Slimy Sid reeled back.

"Me? Would I . . . ? Why *me*? Why not Dogface Dick or the No-Nose Kid, they'd steal their mom's last dollar, the dirty . . ."

He never finished.

Or if he did, nobody could have heard him.

For twelve guns were out and blasting, muzzle flame spearing the blackness, bullets whanging around the rock like mad steel bees. Arthur dropped as quick as light below his rock, curled like a hedgehog, tight as he could, small as he could, against the flying lead.

And when it had stopped, he waited for some time before lifting his head, and even longer before looking out.

Through the smoke-writhing darkness, he could just make out the six still shapes lying around the great pile of loot they would not be spending now.

Quickly, not looking down, and not looking back, Arthur ran through the cave, toward the sunlight and the horses.

The ride to Junction City was not quite as far as Arthur had anticipated, since the gang had doubled back to their hideout from the ambushed train; but, even so, it was almost thirty miles, and Arthur, wearier than he had ever felt in all his life, did not arrive until the last of the evening sun was slanting his long shadow before him down Main Street.

The first person he saw was Herbert McPhoon, who immediately fainted.

Indeed, it was the noise of Herbert McPhoon hitting the ground (he was carrying a tray of egg salad sandwiches from the Railroad Hotel to the jail, for reasons which will become clear in a moment) which made everyone on the street look round.

And when they did, they staggered!

Some went white!

And they all started shouting!

"Run for your lives!" they cried, doing just that, and "It's Railroad Arthur!" and "Hide the trains!" and "He's come back to kill us all!" and many more similarly crazy and panicky cries as they fled from the small figure whom they firmly believed to have committed four daring holdups, and who must now be riding in at the head of his gang to perpetrate something even more terrible.

As they fell back, shrieking, before his horse, Arthur rode slowly up to the sheriff's office, dismounted, tied his horse to the hitching post, and walked through the door.

He caught the sheriff at a particularly unfortunate moment. The sheriff was standing at an ironing-board, in his long woolly underwear, pressing his best flannel trousers. His guns — not, as you know, that he was much use with them — were hanging on a peg across the room.

"Yes?" inquired the sheriff, not looking up (he was having some difficulty getting the crease right at the knee).

"Good evening," said Arthur.

Slowly, as if hoping against hope that he would not see what he knew, deep down, he was going to see, the sheriff looked up.

"Aaaaargh!" he screamed, the iron falling from his fingers.

"It's all right," said Arthur, "I have come to

tell you that I have solved the railroad robberies and recovered all the loot. And also to
tell you how to get to the gang's hideout so that
you can pick it up."

"But — but —" stammered the sheriff, his
face as chalk-pale as his underpants, "— *you*
did all the robberies!"

"Wrong," replied Arthur, as simply as that,
"and this proves it."

Suddenly, a third voice joined in.

"What's happening?" it cried. "What's
going on? Who's there?"

"Goodness me!" exclaimed Arthur. "Is that
Mr. Beesley?"

"We locked him up," said the sheriff, "after
this morning's robbery. The railroad company
suggested it. They reckoned that you had to
have had an accomplice in Junction City, what
with the mail car being uncoupled and every-

thing, and Mr. Beesley seemed to be the man you knew best. It was all very suspicious."

"Never have suspicions," said Arthur sternly, looking the sheriff straight in the eye, "without very good reasons. You can do a lot of damage, going around suspecting everyone."

"Are those my egg salad sandwiches?" cried the wretched Mr. Beesley. "I'm starving!"

Arthur walked through to the very same cell in which he had spent the previous day. The stationmaster reeled back from the bars.

"YOU!" he cried. And then his expression changed from terror to supplication. His face went soggy, a tiny tear appeared in each eye. "Look," he wheedled, "I know you're a terrible villain and everything, but I did let you stand on my bridge. Won't you tell them I had nothing to do with it?"

"I'll do better than that," said Arthur. "I have recovered all the stolen property, I have got the entire gang where they will do no more harm, and I have drawn a map so that you can go and see for yourself. I would lead you there personally," he added, "except that I not only didn't get much sleep last night, I also missed my bath, and would rather like to go home."

Mr. Beesley sat down on the bed, hard. He could not believe what he had just heard!

"Get me out of here!" he snapped, standing up, and quite becoming his old self again. "We must go across to the station! The railroad company bosses are all there holding an inquiry; any minute now they'll probably appoint a new stationmaster!"

Arthur was too polite to remark that this was not perhaps the most important aspect of the whole business. He merely nodded, and went to ask the sheriff to unlock the cell door.

The sheriff was still standing where Arthur had left him, staring glazedly at the wall. He handed Arthur the keys as if in a dream, not saying a word. Arthur tugged his sleeve.

"There's just one other thing," he murmured.

The sheriff looked slowly down.

"What's that?" he said.

"Your trousers," said Arthur. "I'm afraid they seem to be glowing."

The sheriff jumped!

The iron remained where he had dropped it, and a big iron-shaped hole, smoldering at the edges, had burned itself into the smart, expensive seat.

★

"Incredible! Amazing! Astounding!"

With these and many other exclamations the assembled railroad bosses greeted the end of Arthur's story. Four fat pink-faced gentlemen in identical brown suits, they had sat rapt throughout, their mouths dropping more and more open with each new remarkable detail.

"It is truly astonishing!" announced the president after the assembled townspeople, who were all present in the enormous waiting-room for the inquiry, had finished applauding and cheering. "Do you realize that this magnificent achievement could have been pulled off only *by a small boy?* Only a small boy could have escaped from the jail, only a small boy could have hidden himself inside a mailbag, only a small boy, in short, could have saved us all from the disaster that threatened both the company and the town!"

"Hurrah!" cried the citizens. "Hurrah for Arthur!"

"Only a boy would have collected train numbers, too," said another director of the company, "and I've been wondering just where they fitted in. You told us," he said, turning to Arthur with a broad and kindly smile, "that the train numbers gave you your first clue."

"That's right," said Arthur, opening his red notebook. "You see, I happened to notice that the first three numbers of each of the ambushed trains were the same — 245889, 245673, and 245313. I then looked back in my notebook and saw that the next train to have a 245 number would be Friday's nine-thirty to Weasel Fork, number 245777, which I'd written down the Friday before."

"Remarkable!" cried the president. "But what made the gang select 245 numbers in the first place?"

"Gangs," said Arthur, "always work to a pattern. That is one of the things about gangs."

Everyone nodded.

"I always said train-watching was a fine hobby," said the bank manager, without even a blush.

"There will, of course, be a reward," said the president, "but I think that the company should also do something rather special to commemorate this stirring adventure." He cleared his throat, which he always did before making particularly important speeches. "As you have heard, all trains have numbers. What you may not know — although I'm certain Arthur's sharp eyes will not have missed it, ha! ha!

ha! — is that most engines also have names. Tomorrow, a new nameplate shall be struck for the engine that pulled today's nine-thirty to Weasel Fork: henceforth, it shall be called RAILROAD ARTHUR!"

How the cheers rang out! How the massed feet stamped! And how, even though his face showed only a grateful and courteous smile, Arthur's heart seemed to jump about inside him with delight!

But perhaps the most remarkable thing of all was that Herbert McPhoon stole quietly away from the noisy gathering, stepped smartly across to the bell tower, and suddenly filled the sunset countryside with loud and continuous bonging!

He had no idea, of course, how he would explain it (since there was no train coming) to the company. But, for once, he didn't worry about it for one moment!